Our Small Faces

A Novelette
by
Jamie L. Moore

Copyright © 2013 Jamie L. Moore
Cover Art © 2013 by Rachel Annette Blodgett
ELJ Publications

All rights reserved.

ISBN: 978-0615911588

DEDICATION

To my mother, Theresa, for always supporting me through everything and believing in my writing. To my uncle, Donald (Skip) Brown, for your continued encouragement.

ACKNOWLEDGMENTS

Thank you to the publications that have given this work a chance, including *Emerge Literary Journal* and *Blackberry: A Magazine*. Thank you to my writing communities/residencies/workshops that have blessed me with friends and motivators that stretch across the literary worlds. To my mentors at Antioch University Los Angeles - Alma Luz Villanueva and Tananarive Due - for guiding me through my manuscript in all its forms. To my mentors, Heidi Durrow and Susan Bono, for being the first people to give my voice a platform. Lastly, to those in my hometown of Santa Rosa, for giving me history, purpose and place.

Selma

Island

My momma had a picture of my grandmother above the fireplace. Grandmother looked like a regal woman: chin held high, slight mysterious smile, hair tucked into a wide black hat. The picture was taken in 1949, just a few years before her first child, my uncle, was born. Thirty years later, she was long gone and laid to rest in Georgia, in the town Momma grew up in. Now we were far from Georgia, tucked into a Northern California valley. Our town was the kind that snubbed the city radicals just below us; the muted suburbia of Daddy's dreams. As much as Daddy liked our fenced in plots, he said it wasn't the place his Black Panther brother had written him about. He'd gone about sixty miles too far north to witness the revolution.

All the people that looked like us lived in the same neighborhood, the southeast side, in rows of cul-de-sac roads. My best friends, Zeke Jones and Leroy Jenkins, and I lived in three adjacent houses, mine to the left. My house was the house with peeling pink paint that began the half-circle. To the right was Zeke's white house, and beyond that, Leroy's sponge-cake yellow one had the same clapboard shape as ours. When looking at all three together, it made me think of the layers of a parfait dessert I'd seen in the windows of the kind of fancy restaurants I wasn't supposed to go into. Our houses were separated by scratchy straw patches that might have been grass a long time ago. Around the Jenkins's house, patches of flowers struggled to grow. This place was South Park. South Park was my whole life.

Momma likes to say that her mother would've loved me. But I wonder if she'd even recognize me. My wide nose compared to her slender one, her delicate lips to my full ones. Her skin, like Momma's, looked as light as the paper the picture was printed on. They called her yellow. Nothing like my brown. The only thing I carried of hers was small, even eyes.

On good nights, Daddy would put on a Billie Holiday record and he and Momma would dance in the living room beneath that picture while I sat on the couch convinced this was what love looked like. Momma laughed as Daddy spun her around to her favorite song, "Trav'lin Light." The starched cotton of her dress remained close to her body despite the movement. Momma's laugh was quiet – you had to be looking at her face to know she was laughing. Her mouth became tense, lips pursed and slanted up to the left as her chin bobbed up and down. As they moved, sometimes her stockings slipped against the hardwood floor, but Daddy was quick to catch her. When Momma started to get tired, she'd talk about all the things that needed fixing.

"George, when you gonna clean out that fireplace so we can use it?" she asked, nodding towards the crumbling brick, soot-covered opening.

"Sometime before winter, My Sweet," he answered, pulling her close to touch cheeks. Daddy looked towards Grandmother's picture and I heard him whisper, "Beautiful runs in your family." If he was facing the right way, he'd catch my eye and wink. Like he meant to say I was beautiful too, but I didn't believe him. I was different.

Leroy and I invented a game called Island. We'd walk out to the street at the edge of the neighborhood. E Street, a two lane strip of asphalt, separated us from the backside of the county fairgrounds. Just over the fence was the horse track, the dust from which blew over in little clouds when it was windy, leaving a film on our windows and burning our eyes. The street curved around a parking lot a few feet past Johnny B's Corner Store. Of course in real life we'd gone past that curve many times: to school, to the department store, to the market for something Johnny B's didn't carry. But in our game, everything past that point was a foreign, scary world. Beyond the sidewalk, the street dissolved into water – a moat of monsters that wanted to eat little brown children. Our howling was heard down the block. Whoever was It ran up and down the street to avoid being captured. If caught, they could be thrown into the water to either be eaten or float away to the other world.

"I heard there are aliens out there! Who knows what will happen to me?"

"They'll put you in a cage and poke sticks at you." Zeke said.

"Nope, they'll boil you up in one of those cauldrons like Halloween witches." I added.

Leroy clung to the telephone pole, which was base. He wrapped his arms and legs around it, scooting upwards. He yelled out when Zeke and I grabbed his torso. "Cheating! That's cheating," he called out. We pulled until Leroy gave out, collapsing and sending all three of us tumbling onto the concrete.

All tired out, we'd walk to Johnny's to get candy. Sometimes we'd sit outside on the bus stop bench. I always sat in the middle. When we sat like that, quiet and focused on our lollipops, it felt like the whole world was still with us.

We didn't play the game anymore, but Zeke, Leroy and I still met on the corner. We drank sodas, gazed across the street and sat in that permanent feeling. Legs crossed, Leroy bobbed his ankle up and down, his pants always a little bit too short. Zeke rubbed his fingers over his buzzed scalp and sometimes reached over to touch the end of my braids. No cars passed by. The sun hung low with the tree branches, hugging the hillside. With his door propped open, we heard the *swish* of Johnny sweeping as he got ready to close up. Everything stayed the same here, no matter the outside.

Zeke

Notebook

During our first day of sixth grade, Leroy and I looked over the playground. Everything seemed smaller than before. We sat on top of the metal jungle gym at the edge of the play structures, our bottoms each covering a hexagon plate where the bars bolted together. Our legs swung in the empty space between the bars, Leroy's sharp kneecap jabbing my calf. From our high point, we could see the whole yard, past the yellow line that split the blacktop in half. Across the way, there was a separate fenced in area where the younger kids played, chucking fistfuls of wood chips into each other's hair. They still had the loud voices and energy of summer, while on our side the 4th, 5th and 6th graders knew this was first long, boring day of the next nine months of long, boring days. One kid scuffed his shoes along the four square lines, missing the ball on purpose. Two girls from our class hung on opposite ends of the monkey bars by their elbows, forearms limp and bodies sagged like the scarecrows at the pumpkin patch. September hadn't given up into autumn yet, so no one ran races to keep warm. Even the yard duty, a short, round woman we secretly called Beachball, sat at edge of the timeout bench looking tired. She polished her whistle with the edge of her pastel striped shirt, waiting for chaos to break loose.

Leroy reached in his pocket and pulled out a book just bigger than his palm.

"What's that?"

"This is the notebook that I write about girls in," he said with a smug smile. "One night, when my Father was drinking with Johnny B at my house, I heard them talk about how when they were kids they used to keep a book with all the girls names in them, how pretty they were and if they wanted to go out with them. I thought it was a funny idea."

"Can I see it?" He passed me the thin black notebook. Inside, each page had three rows of girls' names. The first one I read was his entry for Maurette Jones:

Name: Maurette Jones
Top: Small like Grapes
Bottom: Mudpie Flat
Hair: Poop Brown
Reminds me of: A Gopher

"What are you talking about, top and bottom?" I shut the book and gave it back to him.

"You know, like her breasts," he whispered, gesturing like he was holding a ball against his chest. "The stuff men look at on women."

"But most of the girls haven't grown like that yet." I laughed, but Leroy tapped his book proudly.

"You see, that's why I wrote everything in pencil. Everyone changes, especially since we go to middle school next year. Like Laura Perkins, look."

He flipped it open to the page with Laura's name. The page was a bit smeared from eraser marks and in dark print after "Top" was written: *Round like Oranges*. I laughed with him.

"Here, I have an extra one," Leroy said. He jumped down from the jungle gym and ran to the edge of the blacktop where all our backpacks sat in a line. The straps of his black backpack were attached with duct tape after he broke them off last year. We both had parents who wouldn't buy new things unless they absolutely had to. Leroy unzipped the top, reached in and pulled out a miniature sized composition book. "It's not the same as mine, but it will work."

I took it and immediately felt a tingle near my belly; that hot feeling
I got when I did something wrong.

Tee, my little brother by two years, came running up to us. He was much more social than me, and spent most of his recess running between groups of people, already friends with the kids in his grade. Momma had let him wear his favorite shirt to school that morning: a light blue T-shirt with a large pocket at the chest just big enough to fit his toy soldier. He held it steady in the pocket as he ran; a hand over his heart like he was coming to break some bad news.

"Zeke, are you going to walk me to the park after school today?" He swatted at a fly that landed on his shiny, broad forehead.

"I already told you yes this morning." I watched while Tee and Leroy slapped palms in a complicated hand jive they made up days ago. Tee messed up an elbow bump and Leroy threw up his arms.

"Got you, Tee! I knew you wouldn't remember!"

I was only a little jealous that they had something special between them.

I looked at my new notebook. I scanned the playground again, looking at the sixth grade girls in a new way. Opening to the first page, I picked up my pencil and wrote:

Name: Selma Brown

Top: Enough

Bottom: Good

Hair: Braids

Reminds me of: The sun or a flower.

Playground

I stood outside Tee's classroom waiting for the bell to ring. The door to his room was the same dark blue as everyone else's, but Mrs. Henry had cut out a tree and taped it to the front. Each leaf of the tree, cut out in a light green color, had a kid's name on it. I found Tee's leaf right near the middle. As I reached out to touch it, the door swung forward and clicked into the open position. Tee skipped out, dragging his sweater on the ground behind him. He dropped his backpack at my feet like I was going to carry it and sniffed a bullet of clear mucus back into his nose.

"Park time! Park time!" he said.

I made him gather all his stuff and we headed away from the school. Soon after, I heard a scuffling behind us. A squeaky call, "Tee, wait up," turned us both around.

Peter waved and rushed to catch up with us. Droplets of sweat dotted his hairline. I thought of Peter as Tee's White Friend, which didn't sound very nice, but Pop did it too: *Tee, is your white friend coming to your birthday picnic?* There wasn't many black kids at our school, (none in Tee's grade), and all of us hung out with each other. I thought Peter and Tee were friends because he was poor like us, and he was loud and unashamed in a way that bothered the other kids. Today he wore a red long sleeved shirt with a penny-sized hole at shoulder. His once-white shoes had dulled to a concrete color; they were the same shoes he had in second grade. The other kids teased him, but it didn't seem to faze Peter much. He just avoided them and followed Tee around like he was led by a string.

Luckily, Olive Park wasn't crowded. The big oak trees that bordered the park were just beginning to show the yellow tint of fall. The seasons in Santa Rosa usually felt behind compared to Chicago. Fall lasted until almost Christmas, and the season after that was Rain. Pop said it didn't even count as winter.

I still remembered the snow of the big city, and the wind that felt like it would slice your throat if you had your mouth open. My family moved to Santa Rosa three years ago. Momma said Pop couldn't
support us trying to chase his music dreams. We rode two long nights through the west half of the country, stopping for one afternoon at Pop's friend's house in Liberal, Kansas. The only thing I remembered about the trip was Mr. and Mrs. Haynes's place. They gave us ham

sandwiches for lunch. Their house smelled like fresh butter, a creaminess in the air that made me feel full. Mrs. Haynes wore a checkered dress the color of sand, and spoke to us with a quiet southern drawl. The rest was a blur of lights and hushed discussion between Pop and Momma. Pop would have a real job working at a lumber factory, thanks to his friend Johnny B, who settled in Santa Rosa with his family years ago. It didn't look like much of a place when we arrived. South Park, our new neighborhood, had no streetlights except on the major street leading in, and low hanging electric lines. "At least it is a house," Pop told us, compared to our old, tiny, city apartment.

Usually I'd be chasing Tee around the swings, but I had a book report due and lots of reading left. My book, *Sounder*, told the story of a black sharecropper family and their hunting dog. It made me wonder if any of my family had ever worked as sharecroppers. Pop's family had lived in the north for a long time, but Momma had roots in the South. She didn't know much about her family past my grandparents. The boy in the book didn't have a name, and he had troubles with racism. I imagined he looked like me or Leroy or Tee. Sometimes he didn't feel worthy of being around. I felt like the boy sometimes.

"C'mon Tee!" I called, as he launched himself from the swing set, landing butt-first in the sand. He waved goodbye to Peter, who was trying unsuccessfully to run up the slide from the wrong end. When Peter looked up, he lost his footing and his body slammed against the hard plastic slide. His head bounced off the edge, and he rolled onto his back. But after a few tense seconds, he stood up, spit out some blood and poked at his mouth.

"Another loose tooth!" he shouted as Tee and I started our walk.

Selma

Beautiful

Walking down South E Street, I noticed the trees bowed over the sidewalk like awnings, giving a pathway of shade. Momma had sent me to the big store to pick up some special things that Johnny B's didn't carry: cake flour, powdered sugar, some spices. I'd made the walk there and back by myself several times, but she always told me to be careful since it was just outside "our side" of town. I was trying to walk quietly, but between the dead leaves beneath me and the crinkling of my two paper bags, I was making as much noise as when I crunched my cereal in the morning. Even though it was pretty to walk down this street that autumn turned orange and red, I usually held my breath until I made it all the way down to Aston – to the street that folded into right where I belonged. I'd never had any problems, until today.

Whoosh. As I passed a small alleyway between buildings, a bike sped up from behind and whipped around me to fast I almost lost my balance. A chubby kid stopped his bike right in front of me, blocking the sidewalk. He looked a little bit older than me, maybe an eighth grader. In his left hand, he held a can of chew with the label torn off. He spit towards his feet, trying to be tough, but he missed the ground. A wad of watery brown tobacco hit his knee and then slid down his pale shin. The juice collected at the top of his tube sock and stained the top a dirty yellow. He dropped his bike to the side and shook out his foot.

"Stupid shit!" he yelled – words I wasn't allowed to use – and his curses stung my ears.

"Hey, Timmy, slow down!" called another kid from behind me. He screeched his bike to a stop, rustling the leaves. He looked at me, blue eyes peeking out between pink, puffy lids. He rubbed at his face. "You know I've got allergies and you kicked all the dust in my face." This boy looked like a skinner version of Where's Waldo in a red and white striped shirt that clung to him so tight I could almost count his rib bones. "What the hell you doing?"

"Tryna see what this bitch is carrying." Timmy answered, walking towards me.

Trouble was thick in the air now. I clutched the bags to my chest and tried to quickly get around him. He pushed me back with ease. It surprised me how quickly kids that seemed harmless one minute turned mean in another. Part of me wanted to laugh at this fat kid spitting on himself and his stick figure friend. I wasn't dumb enough to start a fight. This was why we always had to be careful – this was why I liked to stay at home. All I wanted was to get home.

I stomped on the big one's foot, but as he reeled backward, the other one's sharp elbow jabbed into my stomach and I fell to the ground. The bags spilled forward; all of Momma's Sunday pie supplies scattered at their feet. I rolled over, and the air sliced at my newly-skinned knees.

"Nothing good here," Timmy decided.

"We could still have some fun," said the other, nodding towards me.

He swung back his leg to kick me, and I as braced for the impact, I heard someone run up and push the skinny kid away from me. They started to yell at each other. I scooted back against the wall, tucking my head behind my knees. I scrunched myself together and hoped they'd forget I was here. When I looked up again, the bullies were riding off on their bikes and the boy who was left set the bags, with all of my stuff inside, next to me.

"Are you okay?" he asked, offering a hand to pull me up.

"I think so," I said. I let him help me up and then quickly grabbed the bags. "Thanks," I added before turning away.

"Wait," he said. "I'm Mark. What's you rname? Do you live around here?"

I paused. He looked about thirteen, maybe a year older than me. He wore the same kind of dark blue shirt Zeke had, with a tiny sailboat sewn on the chest. "Selma. South Park."

"Cool." He scuffed his shoe on the sidewalk, then looked at me as he scratched at his blond hair. "You're kinda beautiful."

I almost laughed again. Beautiful seemed like a grown-up word. It made me feel both big and small at the same time. I tried to be polite so I could leave. "Thanks."

"Can I see you again?"

My heart sputtered in my chest like Pop's pickup truck when it wouldn't start. Firstly, I knew I wasn't supposed to be talking to boys who my parents didn't know. Second, I wasn't supposed to talk to boys if I didn't know if they went to church or not. And third, I especially wasn't supposed to talk to stranger, non-church white boys.

"Sundays, in the afternoons," I started before my brain caught with me, "I go to get a soda at Johnny's Corner Store with my allowance."

"Johnny's – the one down the street?" He asked, pointing in the direction of my neighborhood.

"Yeah."

He smiled and crossed the street, walking back the way he came. "Maybe I will see you there," he called.

Zeke

Thrifty's

We had only been to Thrifty's on weekends with Momma and Pop when the old man worked behind the counter. The old man was bald, and his plastic name tag said Ed with two gold star stickers next to it. The old man always packed the ice cream tightly as we watched his skinny, grey-haired arms flaws through the glass display case. He strained to make the biggest scoops possible. Maybe that's how he got the gold stars. As long as he had it, Pop always left him an extra tip. The old man placed his hand at his belly over his faded red apron and gave a yellow-toothed thank you smile.

But it a weekday, afterschool, and a teenager stood on duty. His blond hair stood in greasy spikes around the band of his Thrifty's visor. He didn't see us come in – busy talking to two other teenager boys that seemed to be his friends. All three of them had a sallow look about them under the florescent store lights. Tee ran straight up to the ice cream freezer, placing his hands and forehead on the glass to look down at the cardboard barrels of flavors. One of friends noticed us then, motioning to the visor guy. The other friend said "Aww, shit," before standing up, pulling a thinly rolled cigarette out of pocket and heading outside.

"Put your money up here first," Visor said, standing behind the cash register. I slid my two quarters across the counter. As he picked them up, I noticed he wasn't wearing the plastic gloves like the old man wore; his fingertips dingy from smoking or maybe tobacco.

Tee pointed to the flavor on the far left, "This one, Zeke."

"One strawberry," I asked, "and one rainbow sherbet, please."

Visor smirked and grabbed a cone from the dispenser behind him. Without using the ice cream scooper, he scraped the cone inside the strawberry barrel, smashing the edges of the cone. Tee made a yelping noise like a puppy with its tail caught. I pinched his side to make him shut up. When Visor pushed the cone across the counter, I saw that not more than two tablespoons of ice cream had made it inside. Visor looked me in the eye, daring me to protest, but I handed the cone to Tee without a word. I made a quick glance around the rest of the store

– past the candy aisle, over by the cough medicine – but no one was around. When my cone was placed on the counter, the top part of it had broken off. Inside was a yellowy-white ice cream with brown flakes. Inside the ice cream case, there were pieces of soggy cone stuck inside the flavor next to rainbow sherbet. Butter pecan. I hated butter pecan. It was an old person flavor, like something Pop would order. Visor wiped his hands on his jeans and turned back to his friend.

"Let's go, Tee," I said, grabbing my half cone and pushing my little brother towards the door. Tee made it out a few steps ahead of me, so that I watched a foot pop out in front of him. Tee tripped, luckily keeping himself and his ice cream from falling.

"Leave him alone!" I shouted before I saw who it was. The guy with the cigarette stepped in front of me.

"Or what?" he said.

I didn't want him to know I was shaking. I knew my voice would give it away. He was bigger, and I didn't have a chance of getting anything past him. In school, they told us if someone bullied you, to ignore them, and they'd go away. I hoped by not saying anything, he'd get bored and move out of my way. Instead, he grabbed my ice cream, and tipped it back over his mouth, slurping down the tiny bit of butter pecan inside. He dropped the empty cone on the sidewalk and crushed it under his black boot. It made the same quick crunch as that time when Leroy stepped on a beetle. When I tried to move around him, he hit me square in the mouth, not as hard as he could have, but he had a ring on his finger that caught my bottom lip and split it like a skirt seam.

I was not going to cry in front of cigarette guy. I was not going to cry in front of Tee. I held my mouth and coughed at the copper sting of blood as I grabbed Tee and ran the way home.

Of course when we got home, Momma wanted to know what happened. I didn't want to talk about it, but Tee sang it out like a soloist in a choir. When she told me to uncover my mouth, Momma looked at me with the same faint, squinty face she usually saved for road kill. She cleaned out my lip with alcohol, which burned so bad I thought I was going to rip the tile off the side of the kitchen sink. She spread some Vaseline over it and sent me to my room to lie down.

That happened on a Friday. Two days later, the purpled skin on my lip had started to crust and heal. But it still looked ugly. Momma made me put on my best suit even though it was a regular Sunday service at church. My grey slacks fit a little tight, and since Tee had stolen my belt, I had to wear my white button down tucked in plus my stuffy grey blazer over it. At least my red and blue tie clipped on, so Pop didn't hassle about my sloppy tie skills.

After the opening hymns and prayers, the church secretary gave the usual announcements about bible studies and choir meetings. When she called for news from the congregation, Pop straightened his slacks and stood up.

"Mind if I come up to the front?" he asked. My stomach dropped.

"Go 'head, Brother Jones." She answered.

"Now I know everyone here knows out community has been under attack since we've settled here," he began. "They've sectioned us off in this area like cattle – can't buy property or business space on the other side of town. And one by one, they're kicking down our children. Zeke, come up here."

I didn't move until Momma kicked my shin and pointed to the aisle. Pop had me stand in front of him and placed his hands on my shoulders like we were taking a portrait.

"As everyone can see, Zeke took a hit two days ago, just trying to leave the store. Y'all know my son to be good young man, so this was an attack of malicious intent."

"Mmm-hmm, white devil," I heard Deacon Rig mumble behind us. "I know my son didn't go out to pick a fight did you?"

Pop gripped my shoulder, a cue to answer. "No, sir."

"Didn't try to steal nothing, minded your P's and Q's"

"Yes, sir."

"And this isn't the first time this has happened, many of us and our children have experienced incidents like this."

The grownups were keeping a tally, and I had made the list. Like the time Leroy's sister, Lettie, got her dress torn apart by a group of older girls at school. Or when Donnie's bike and backpack were stolen. Johnny B getting punched downtown. Maurette getting chased out of the park. Or Miss Etta getting harassed at the grocery store.

"I think we draw the line at our children," Pop continued. "No matter what's happening everyone else, we're still fighting a Civil War in this town. I think it's time we reach out to the NAACP, perhaps began our own chapter, and take legal action to secure our rights!"

As the younger ones, the most innocent victims, we were the bridge to our injustice getting noticed. But I was afraid if this was a war like we learned about in school, there would be causalities. That was my teacher's big word for how many people got hurt. If everywhere else was getting better, why couldn't we just wait for change? I saw it on the news – people marching with signs and black people voting. It was happening, it would come. I didn't know N-double A-C-P meant, but it sounded serious. The church responded with resounding "Amens!" I tilted my head backwards to look at him. His face was sharp angles, tight jaw – he didn't look like my Pop. He looked like one of those T.V. people yelling behind a microphone. And we, the children, stood amongst the crowd, looking for answers. We, the small faces of their revolution.

Selma

Date

It was Sunday, and my new dollar was hot in my pocket. I headed to Johnny's. His store had been a little quiet lately. The day Johnny brought a white girl to stay with him, our neighborhood earthquaked with gossip. My own Momma helped lead an emergency prayer session when word spread that Johnny and his new woman would get married in our own church.

"The Devil is upon us Lord," I heard Miss Ruth call from my living room the morning the deacons' wives gathered together. "A snake whispering in the ear of one of our own. We ask for your mercy." They knelt with clasped hands around the coffee table, each wearing some variation on the same calf-length, cotton work dress. The echoing "Amens" were crisp arrows shot from their mouths into the air. I backed into the hallway to miss the line of fire. I didn't understand how love and hate could coexist so purely in their hearts.

Of everyone in my contained world, it seemed Johnny would have the least to say about my secret meeting with Mark.

October had just settled in; the first month here after summer that the breezes get crisp enough for a real jacket. I decided to wear my new winter coat. It looked like fur, even though it was fake, and had silver flecks that glittered like the tinsel on a Christmas tree. My hands sweated in the lined pockets as I walked to Johnny B's, so I shook them out in the cold to dry them. It was some kind of body miracle that my fingertips stayed frozen while my palms felt like the electric red of stovetop coils.

Mark was already inside the shop by the time I arrived, seated at the bench across from the register. I paused a few steps outside the door to watch him. He wore the standard uniform of a boy from a farming family: light denims and boots, bright button-up shirt that was tucked in. His heavy, brown jacket draped over his lap and he fingered the ribbed cuff. Mark's hair hung around his face in short chunks in the same shape a child draws ocean waves. At his feet, two bottles of soda sweated a puddle onto Johnny's wood floor.

Johnny greeted me with a half-smile, nodding to where Mark sat. In the corner of my eye, I caught a shadow down the first aisle of the small store, but didn't think much of it. Mark stood up to briefly hug me, and we sat together on the bench.

"I got you a root beer, is that what you like?" Mark spoke with lots of pauses, like he thought through every word. His eyes weren't eager, but inquisitive, patient.

"That's perfect," I said, the other sounds around me dulling except his voice. I could've lived in that oblivion forever.

We drank our sodas and took a short walk behind the business buildings. We passed one big, blue dumpster after another in the alleyway just wide enough for the city dump truck. Mark held my hand for balance as I tightrope-walked the sidewalk curbs. I told him about the old ladies who always fell asleep during church in the pew in front of me. I told him about midterms, and lunches with Zeke and Leroy. I told him about how I wanted to be a nurse, even after my teacher told me to forget about science.

"You can do whatever you want to do," he said, suddenly lifting me at waist and turning in a circle, "Look, you can even fly."

***

Zeke and Leroy stood at the corner of our street, Pressely Drive, like they had been waiting for me. I grinned like it was normal, and waved.

"Whew, it's cold. What are you two doing?" I asked, stuffing my hands in my pockets.

"We were helping Johnny B in the store. Interesting, we saw you there." Leroy answered. My smile faded. My chest felt heavy. They were the shadow in store. "You can't say anything. You can't tell my mother. It was nothing, just my friend."

"More than that," Zeke muttered, staring at my shoelaces.

"Don't say that like you know." I shot back, and my throat closed up.

"Well, I won't say nothing," Leroy started. "But you got to do something for me."

"What?" I said.

"Go with me to the dance at school. Be my date." Leroy smirked. He nudged Zeke hard with his elbow, but I felt that jab, right near the ribs. We had a winter formal at our school, one fancy dance like they had at the middle school, no little kids allowed.

Later that afternoon, I walked over to Zeke's house, where he sat on the porch looking through old music sheets. I knew they belonged to his father, and that Zeke always wanted to learn how to play. But his father didn't want him to catch the music bug and forget school, so he refused to teach him. Zeke wouldn't defy him. He was the kind of person to give up his dreams for someone else.

"Why did you guys hide, why didn't you just say something when you saw me?" I asked him.

"Leroy wanted to see what you were going to do with that guy. He wanted it to be a surprise I guess. Anyway, you shouldn't be hanging out with someone like that. You already know what your mom would say."

"Someone like what, Zeke. Just say it."

He sighed and wouldn't look at my face. "You know, white. It's just… school, church…"

"He's just my friend. It's not like it's 1850. This is why I hate living in this stupid town." My whole body was hot and shaking. I took off my coat and set it down beside me.

Zeke's eyebrows gathered and he leaned in with a quiet voice, "Did you even think for a second why nobody was in Johnny's store on a Sunday? Shopping day? 'Cause half the neighborhood is boycotting anything to do with him except church since he brought her to church. He can't even pay me for my work. I keep going in 'cause he's always been good to me and I can't do him like that. But no one likes it. And we aren't here to change the rules." He pulled at the skin around his fingernails, a nervous habit I recognized from the first time we met at elementary school. "Why are you hanging out with him?"

I told Zeke what happened on my walk home that day.

Zeke sat there waiting, knowing there was more. "And?"

"I think I like him. He told me I was beautiful, okay?"

Zeke jumped up and began to stuff the music sheets back into a folder. "But why would you meet him by yourself like that? You don't know him. Is that all it takes? Some stranger to say you're pretty?"

I stood up beside him, matched his height. "No! Don't try to make me out to be some loose girl." My tongue felt heavy and thick as I walked down the porch steps.

Zeke

Hollow

Every year, in the late fall, Pop liked to go camping on his birthday weekend. This time we didn't go far; we hiked the trails of the big state park where people could hunt small game. Just the night earlier, Tee had spotted a shooting star, and pointing it out to all of us, wished aloud to see a mountain lion with his own eyes.

"So foolish," whispered Momma feverishly, "I'm sure a mountain lion wouldn't mind seeing you either. It would see you fit for a nice snack."

By midday, we reached a flat area in a grove of trees that Pop decided was as good as any place to stop for lunch. Tee and I threw our knapsacks in a pile, circling the trunks of trees in a haphazard game of tag. Three or so squirrels skittered about, snatching fallen acorns.

"Hey Pop, can I shoot at a squirrel?" Tee asked. Pop was busy reading one of his camping manuals and didn't hear him. Tee ran back over to our pile of stuff, and hustled through Pop's bag until he pulled out our father's small hunting gun from its special black case. I watched him react to the weight of it, sliding his fingers along the gun's exterior. Holding it at the trigger just like Pop did, Tee closed one eye, and pointed it around, mouthing *bang boom*. He smiled over to me, tucked the barrel of the gun into the pocket of his denim jeans, and began to run in my direction, his fingers still interlaced in the loophole near the trigger.

Tee tripped on a rock. Surprised tension froze his body. The noise was deep and sharp; the last outside sound I heard before the *doom doom* pounding of my heart closed off my ears. I watched Tee's jaw go slack from the shock, watched his muscles and bones fold up on each other as he crumpled onto the straw-colored grass. Momma and Pop must have yelled, and by the time I blinked, both were kneeling beside him. Momma pointed Pop over to the path, and he ran off for help, only one arm in his white sweater; the rest flapping behind him like a flag.

As I inched closer, she lifted Tee's head to her lap, pulling his leg out enough that I could see the waves of molasses-thick blood leaking from his left thigh. Again, my heart: *doom doom doom*, deafened me. His chest heaved in and out in shaky breaths. I watched Momma whisper into his ear, blowing the wet trails of his tears dry against his cheeks until Pop returned.

At the hospital they told us he'd lost so much blood they couldn't work fast enough to save him. Pop had to grasp Momma by the waist to keep her up when her legs went loose. He held her there, lightly kissed the back of her neck and hid his face in her hair while he cried. I sat on the floor of the waiting room, my body pulsing with hollowness like an organ had been ripped straight from my middle.

At Tee's funeral, most everyone from the neighborhood was there. I watched each family file in; the few kids I played with suddenly quiet, taking their seats quickly as if to avoid me. The Browns came, and there was Selma, in a black dress and patent leather shoes.

Pastor Donald, the one Tee made fun of for his stutter, gave the opening prayer. After a hymn from the five members of the ladies' chorus, Pastor Donald called up anyone who wanted to say anything. Tee's third grade teacher took the podium, saying he was a good student, and friend to everyone. Mrs. Brown said some nice things that made Momma cry.

I looked down at my fingers for the next few people until I heard Leroy's voice on the microphone. When I lifted my head to look, there he was at the pulpit, in a blue button down shirt with some dirt on the left elbow, half-smiling to the audience.

"Tee was my friend. Sometimes he acted worse than me, sometimes I was worse than him. Actually we were pretty even. I liked to throw stones into the storm pipe with him and Zeke. I wanted to go with him fishing one day like he said he did with his Pop, but now it will be different. I think Tee is out fishing somewhere up there." As Leroy stepped down, he noticed me looking at him and motioned his head towards the door.

I turned to my Pop, "I have to go to the bathroom."

He nodded, and I followed Leroy's path to the lobby.

"Let's leave," Leroy said to me, tapping his foot.

"I can't just leave," I started. "What about my parents?"

"After this is done then." He turned and walked back inside, taking his place next to his little sister in the third pew. As I walked backed to my seat, I felt pairs of eyes following me. The ladies choir rose again and began singing "This Little Light of Mine."

Momma held me by my shoulders as I sat down, kissing my earlobe, "You're my last little light, baby. My last one."

I wondered when it would stop feeling like I was sinking.

Leroy was waiting for me outside on the steps, his shirt already unbuttoned halfway, showing a white sleeveless undershirt.

"Are you coming with me?" he asked, with the same half-smile that showed just a peek of his top teeth. I knew exactly where we were going.

I slipped off my dress shoes at the edge of the creek, and draped my socks over them. Leroy and I climbed through the bushes into the little valley where the open mouth of a large steel pipe met the marshy grass and mud. Since the inside of it was mostly dry, we crouched there, leaning on the interior walls. Leroy reached into one of his pockets, emptying the stones he'd picked up on the walk to the creek into my cupped hands. One by one, we threw the smooth rocks down the length of the pipe toward the dark, shadowy pit that echoed *ting ting ting* as the rocks traveled beyond the reach of the sunlight.

"This doesn't make you feel sad or nothing, does it?" Leroy looked up as he wiped his nose on his sleeve.

"Nah, it's better than that stuffy church." I answered. "Are we real friends? I mean, my Momma asked me who my best friend was and I said you because it just seemed okay, but I didn't really know."

For a moment, I felt a pinch of warmth near my belly like after eating a bowl of soup. I trusted Leroy to be the same to me no matter what. "Yeah, we're real friends."

Selma

Dance

The night of the winter formal, I put on my best dress and Leroy held me on his arm proud. He held open doors, and got me drinks. His hands stayed on my hips as we danced and he didn't make any dumb jokes. As we moved, one step right, one step left, I realized I'd never stood this close to Leroy before. Even if his body wasn't, his eyes were bold, and lighter than I remembered, sepia like the edges of old photographs. His face didn't have the sharp edges that Zeke had. His soft, wide nose and his round cheeks lent to his momma still calling him "Babyface" in public. A slow Janet Jackson song came on the stereo system. My hands moved to his shoulders, then clasped around his neck. In the dim light I noticed how my skin blended with his. We were so much of the same. I let Leroy kiss me that night because this was how I was supposed to fall in love.

And then suddenly, without any official declaration, Leroy and I started to go steady. He got a job at Lonnie's Barbershop to pay for our dates. We went for ice cream Saturday nights and movies every other week. It felt natural being with Leroy – this new extension of a friendship I'd had for as long as I could remember. It wasn't exciting like Mark was, but I didn't think of them the same. Mark wasn't a part of this world, and sometimes he didn't even feel real.

Leroy and I could be outside freely, and I wanted to get used to that feeling. My body had a different kind of confidence standing next to Leroy – an ease, a relief at our invisibility together.

Zeke

Love

The night of the winter dance, I sat on my porch, having told everyone that my stomach ached and I was too sick to go. Watching Leroy walk by did make my insides flip-flop. He gave me a nod and smile as he passed. Selma answered the door in a pink dress, her shoulders covered with a black shawl. Her mother had taken out her old braids and twisted new ones, weaving ribbon through her hair. I wanted to believe Leroy had no idea why I was sick. I wanted Selma to have a good time. But I didn't want to be forgotten, stuck in the gray shadows between them.

Momma called Leroy and Selma "a nice little couple". I went to Johnny B's now by myself, while Leroy earned change at the barbershop doing chores. I watched Mark pass by the store once a week on his way to the track to meet her. Despite a small pit of guilt about not telling Leroy, it gave me some hope to have something only I knew. It was the same kind of secret-keeping Leroy used to get her in the first place.

The first day of spring, Leroy brought out his new baseball. We played a game of catch, each trying to throw the ball faster than the other. I pulled my arm back as far as I could without losing my balance, pitching it harder, but way to the right. The side window of Leroy's house shattered as soon as the ball made impact, the sound echoing down the street. Within seconds, Mrs. Jenkins appeared in the doorway, her knobby finger beckoning me to her porch. Knowing I had no money, she and Mr. Jenkins decided I could pull the weeds up around their house as punishment, though Momma thought they were being too nice.

That evening, in the last of warm orange glow from the sun, I started to rip up the dandelion plants by their roots. I noticed the window above my head leading to Leroy's room was open. I heard him open and close the closet, humming some rock and roll song I didn't recognize. Then I heard his father's voice, a low baritone that sounded like the morning announcer on the radio.

"Son, I saw you with the Brown's girl."

"Yes, sir." Leroy's voice sounded meek.

"I hear you're going steady with her." The floorboards groaned, a shift of his weight.

"Yes sir."

"Well, treat 'er right. If you keep it up you might actually get somewhere in life. That girl is goin' places, and she might take you with her. You're going up fast, son, and then you'll need to have a real job and make a family. Just like everyone else." Mr. Jenkins coughed, a deep rattle in his throat from smoking. "Go to sleep now, cut this light off." I heard the door close, and Leroy sigh.

My hands started to itch, and I vomited there in the yellow-green grass, now left in a shadow when the light from Leroy's window disappeared.

"I'm gonna marry her," Leroy told me at lunch in the next day. "That's all."

I set aside my soda, and leaned back in the booth. "But you don't love her," I said, louder than I expected.

"Yes I do," he shot back defensively, not meeting my stare. "It's the right thing to do." I took up my soda again, the carbonation stinging my throat.

    We didn't say much to each other on the walk home. He scuffed his shoes against the sidewalk with every other step, head hanging low and swaying like a willow branch. I knew he was somewhere deep inside his head I couldn't get to.

Selma

Fairgrounds

The fairgrounds sat on the east side of town, nestled right at the edge of our neighborhood. At the other side of the fairgrounds, the streets led further east and uphill, where some of the richer Santa Rosans lived. Leroy didn't spend any money for three weeks so we could go to the fair. After admission, we counted enough money for three rides and a funnel cake to share. Leroy grabbed a map from the gazebo shaped information booth decorated with red and flowers for this year's theme: "A Flower's Salute to Founders." The fair themes existed mostly for the Hall of Flowers, where Leroy and I walked through first. The large, rectangular building was as wide as two basketball courts, filled with garden exhibits that matched the theme. The winning exhibit was placed in the middle of the hall – this year it was a spread of red, white and blue flowers surrounding an aerial diorama of the city. Around the tiny buildings, clay figurines of the first president, the founders of California, and important men of our city stood proud. Little spouts at each side spit jets of water that rainbowed over it all.

"This is boring, let's go to the stables to see the animals," Leroy said.

But I wanted to watch the water shoot across a few more times, back and forth, from one side of town to the other. It looked graceful. Leroy wrapped his arm around me, higher than the waist, so that his thumb brushed the fabric right beneath my breast. Then he turned sideways, pulled me to him and kissed my cheek. He pulled away slowly. I could feel him studying me face as my eyes scanned the space around us. Leroy laughed.

"What?" I asked.

"You made this face after I kiss you. Like your mouth pulled to the side and your eyes looked around. I'm trying to figure out what you're looking at." He turned his neck around in jest, pointing at the different groups of flowers. "This, or that over there?"

The truth was, when Leroy kissed me, all of me emptied out. My brain turned off. Every time he touched me in that way, I felt vacant.

After we visited the 4-H animals in the stables, we stood in the line for a free ice cream cone from the local dairy. While we waited, Leroy saw one of his friends over at a nearby booth.

"Be right back," he said, as he headed over to say hi.

When I was about halfway up in the line, Leroy still wasn't back yet. He'd disappeared around the corner with his friend. The sun started to really bear down and my sandals burned my feet from standing in the same place for too long. Out of nowhere, two chubby white kids, each about a head taller than me, came at me from opposite sides and pinned me between their chests.

"Look, Beau, we made a nigger sandwich!" the kid on the right said to the other, his ice cream cone dripping down his forearm and into my hair.

"That's pretty funny," the other added, "I think she likes it too." The one on the left took the last bit of his uneaten cone and smashed it into my shirt. He used his wide palm to rub in it, pushing against my breasts and down my stomach. His breath was hot and wet in my ear. "Oh, guess I spilled."

"Get off of me!" I yelled, trying to push them away. The person in line before me, an older man in a cowboy hat, only turned around and smirked, then took another step forward in line.

"What's the matter?" the one the right teased, "My daddy said nigger girls like it rough." He thrust his hips at me before they pushed me down and both ran off towards the horse track. The lady who was behind me stepped around and took my place in line.

Leroy came running up and helped me to my feet. He asked what happened, but I just told him I wanted to go home. He used the funnel cake money to bribe his friend to drive us back to my house. I couldn't help but think, even though it was a stupid thought, what would have happened if Mark was there. If he would've left me by myself for even a second. If maybe he could have been there, one more time, to save me.

Zeke

Choose

I started a habit of walking to the old playground by myself. I had listened to grown-ups talk about the good old days, and here I was at thirteen already wishing I could reverse time. Sometimes, when I sat there, Tee's voice came into my head. Tee and I would talk about everyday things, like how much money I saved up working at Johnny's. We talked about the secret things – stuff I didn't tell anyone else that I felt. I told him how empty my insides seemed. I told him about the big argument I had with Leroy when he found the notebook with Selma's name in it. Even though I told him I wrote it before he went out with her, he said I liked her too much, and since we were going to be high schoolers soon, he had to defend his girlfriend.

"What? Did you learn that from your Dad?" I said to him. Leroy punched me then, square in the nose.

"You don't get nobody when you're hanging on to everybody." Tee said to me.

I threw up my hands, "I don't understand."

"You're too busy being everyone's friend to do something for yourself."

"What do I do, Tee?"

"Look up."

"What?" A rush of air swept past me, and as I raised my head I saw her walking towards me.

Selma hid her hands behind her back as she walked up to me, but her head was high. I shifted my weight on the old wooden bench, and looked out onto the muddy field where Leroy and I used to play games of baseball. There they were again, both of them in my head at the same time. They refused to be separated.

"I found you." Selma stood in front of me. She swayed back on her heels for a moment, the fabric of her dress hitting her knees, then swinging out again.

"Didn't know you were looking for me."

"Zeke, come on, I heard you and Leroy had a fight. He said you told him he wasn't doing the right thing with his life and he was going nowhere. I don't understand what is going on."

"He left out a lot," I said. "You don't know what's going on Selma, and maybe that's better."

Selma lowered next to me on the bench, quickly sitting on her hands. "Why don't you tell me," she bumped her elbow against mine.

I felt a wave of cold. She watched me stiffen, and shifted her hip away from me.

"What? You mad at me now? What did I do, Zeke?"

In a single, swift motion, she pulled her hands from out under herself, and folded them in her lap, right over left. I lost my breath for a moment; felt nothing but my heartbeat shudder in my chest. I reached over, lightly grazing the soft spot of skin above her elbow as I traced my fingers down her arm and took her left hand in mine. I moved our hands to my lap, and she scooted closer to me again.

I met her gaze. Her eyes filled. "You fought about me," she said. "Zeke, tell me."

I let go of her hand.

"Tell you what, Selma? That I'm the one who liked you first? That I'm scared that we all suddenly have to be grown-ups? That I've never told Leroy I've still seen you with the white boy? I never wanted to tell you anything, because I never wanted you to choose, or for me to choose."

"Why?"

"Leroy is supposed to be my best friend. You are my friend. Either way I lose somebody, and I've already lost Tee."

Selma crossed her arms. "Only change is coming." She looked down at our hands. "Ask me to choose."

I lost my breath, and coughed. "No."

Selma stood up, leaned over and grabbed my shoulder. "Zeke, I said ask me to choose."

"I can't."

She pushed me so hard I almost fell off the bench. "Then you'll never get the answer you want."

Three days later, I saw Leroy walking in from of Johnny B's. This time he hit me in the mouth. My jaw pulsed with pain – I could feel it swelling.

"Fuck you. She's gone." He swung again, and I ducked. "What did you say to her?"

"Nothing."

Another swing, my stomach went inward with the force. "Liar. You told her to leave me, didn't you?"

"No, I didn't." Blood in my mouth coated my tongue with a metal sting.

"Yes you did, Zeke. She told me it wasn't you or me. Then she left." Leroy sat down on the curb. "I can't have just one good thing. I'm not good at anything. And when you're not smart, you get stuck here." He gestured around, our four city blocks, our segregated island. "I thought if I could keep her, I could maybe get out after high school."

"That wasn't gonna work, Leroy."

"Shut up. You don't have anything either."

"I thought I had you as a friend."

Leroy stood and walked the path home.

Johnny B gave me some ice wrapped in a rag for my face, and told me to wipe all the counters clean before I left. "Never thought the two of you would go sour," Johnny shrugged, having watched it all through the window. "But we all become someone different with time."

"Not me," I replied. "I stayed the same."

"Boy, I'm sure you changed when you met that girl. And you changed when someone else got her. You changed with Tee being gone. The only time when change doesn't happen is when you're hanging on to things – even when they are moving without you." Johnny walked into his small office at the back of the shop.

Wiping dust from each shelf, I tried to think how different tomorrow would be from today. I wondered if this whole time the things that I thought held me up where the things that made me weak.

The silence left behind struck me. Leroy was one of my forever-people, like Selma was to him. This whole neighborhood was our forever. We each had roles to live up to, or down to, before we even had a say for ourselves. That's the small town curse everywhere. We were just a band of kids, inside a neighborhood, inside a town. Our lines were thicker, our borders drawn for us. We were made to believe not to expect anything from ourselves, like Leroy. Or get out, like

Selma. Survive, like me. Our small faces wanted to be the change for our families, our neighborhood. But failure already ate at us. Maybe we all right at the beginning. Maybe we should just stay still.

ABOUT THE AUTHOR

Jamie L. Moore received her MFA in fiction from Antioch University, Los Angeles. She was born and raised between several neighborhoods in Santa Rosa, California. She is an alumna of the Squaw Valley Writers Workshop, VONA, and the Mendocino Writers Workshop. Her work has appeared or is forthcoming in *Moonshot Magazine*, *Emerge Literary Journal*, *Drunk Monkeys*, and *Blackberry: A Magazine*. As a mixed kid, she is obsessed with writing about the spaces between. She expresses this through her blog Mixed Reader and work with the Mixed Remixed festival. She lives in California with her large family and currently works as a community college English professor. This way, she gets to indulge in both of her passions: talking about the written word and bridging cultural connections.

Made in the USA
San Bernardino, CA
13 September 2015